The
Secret Santa

"Look!" Bess cried. "My card is in the shape of a Christmas tree. And there are M&M's on the branches. They look like Christmas lights!"

"That's really cool," Nancy said.

"So where's your card?" Bess asked. "What did *you* get?"

Nancy's desk was right next to Bess's. She looked at her desktop. It was bare.

"Nothing," Nancy said. She got a big lump in her throat. "I guess I got nothing!"

THE
NANCY DREW
NOTEBOOKS®

The Secret Santa

CAROLYN KEENE
ILLUSTRATED BY ANTHONY ACCARDO

SCHOLASTIC INC.

New York Toronto London Auckland Sydney
Mexico City New Delhi Hong Kong Buenos Aires

ISBN 0-439-41981-6

12 11 10 9 8 7 6 5 4 3 2 1   2 3 4 5 6 7/0

Printed in the U.S.A.   40

First Scholastic printing, September 2002

Cover art by Joanie Schwarz

THE SECRET SANTA

1

Nothing for Nancy

Ouch!" Nancy Drew cried. "Who pinched me?" She grabbed at the arm of her red-and-white snowflake sweater and whirled around.

Brenda Carlton was right behind her in the school lunch line.

"Just testing," Brenda said.

"Testing what?" Nancy asked.

"To see if you're awake," Brenda answered.

"Of course I'm awake," eight-year-old Nancy said.

"Really?" Brenda said in a snooty voice. "Well, I just read your story in our class newspaper. It sounds like you sleep in school all the time."

Brenda held up a copy of the newspaper. Nancy's story was on the front page. It was called "My Winter Dream."

"You know why I wrote that," Nancy said. "Ms. Spencer told us to close our eyes and think about anything we wanted. Then she said to write about our daydream. So that's what I did."

"I did that, too," Brenda said. "But I don't see what's so great about your daydream. My story should have been in the paper instead."

Nancy rolled her eyes. "Maybe Ms. Spencer will pick one of your stories next time," she told Brenda. "Just don't pinch me again."

Then Nancy turned around to talk to her best friend Bess Marvin.

"She thinks she knows everything because her father owns a newspaper," Bess whispered.

"I know," Nancy said.

"I wish she weren't standing behind us," Bess whispered even more softly.

"She's trying to listen to everything I say."

Just then George Fayne came up to Nancy and Bess. She was Bess's cousin and Nancy's other best friend. All three girls were in the same third-grade class.

"Hi!" Nancy said in a cheerful voice. "Where have you been?"

"I left my lunch in the classroom," George explained. "I had to go back to get it. And then Ms. Spencer wouldn't let me in the room."

Bess's blue eyes sparkled with excitement. "Because of the Secret Santa gifts?" she asked her cousin.

George nodded. "Ms. Spencer is putting them out now."

Nancy clapped her hands. Everyone was excited about Secret Santa. It was a special three-day gift exchange. It always took place right before Christmas vacation. This was the first day.

The fun had really started on Monday. That was when Ms. Spencer had put everyone's name in a bowl. Then each student drew a name. Nancy got Jason Hutchings.

Now Nancy was Jason's Secret Santa. That meant she was supposed to bring him a gift on three different days.

Today the gift was supposed to be a homemade card.

Tomorrow she was supposed to bring Jason's favorite lunch. Nancy knew what to bring because Ms. Spencer had put a chart on the bulletin board. It listed each student's favorite foods and desserts.

On Friday Nancy was supposed to bring a small gift. It couldn't cost more than a few dollars.

All the treats had to be hidden in paper bags. That way no one could see what anyone else brought to school. And no one would know which present came from which person.

"I wonder who my Secret Santa is," George said.

"I just hope my Secret Santa isn't a boy," Bess said.

4

"I hope *mine* isn't Brenda Carlton!" Nancy said under her breath.

Nancy and Bess went through the lunch line quickly. Then they ate with George. After lunch all three girls hurried outside to play in the snow.

A few minutes later Emily Reeves came dashing across the playground. She was in Nancy's third-grade class, too.

Emily had just started taking gymnastics lessons. At recess she liked to practice the moves she had learned.

Emily held out her arms as she spun toward Nancy. Then she lost her balance on the new layer of snow. She skidded and slid into Nancy. She almost knocked her down.

"Oooh! Sorry!" Emily said.

"That's okay," Nancy told her.

"Uh-oh, I hope you're not my Secret Santa," Emily said. "Because now you'll be mad at me and you won't bring me anything nice tomorrow."

5

"Take it easy, Emily," George said. "No one's mad at you."

But Emily wasn't listening. "Can we go inside yet?" she asked. "I can't wait to see my present."

Nancy, George, and Bess laughed. Emily could never wait for anything. They watched as Emily practiced some more moves.

Then Emily said, "I can't wait anymore. I'm going back to the classroom." She headed for the door.

Nancy shook her head. "The bell will ring soon," she said. "She should have waited."

"I know," Bess agreed.

The three friends hopped up and down, waiting for the bell to ring. They were cold—and Nancy was excited, too.

She could hardly wait to find out what her Secret Santa had given her. And she wanted to see Jason's face when he opened the card she had made.

Finally the bell rang. All the kids ran to the door. Some of them pushed and shoved to get inside, including Brenda Carlton.

"Come on," Bess said. "Everyone else is getting there first. I want to see the cards!"

The assistant principal, Mrs. Oshida, had been waiting in the doorway. She walked the class back to their room.

Nancy, Bess, and George hurried to their cubbies outside the room. They took off their mittens, hats, scarves, coats, and boots. Nancy's boots were hard to get off, so she was the last one done.

Finally Nancy walked into the class. Ms. Spencer closed the door behind Nancy.

"Look!" Bess cried as Nancy passed her desk. "My card is in the shape of a Christmas tree. And there are M&M's on the branches. They look like Christmas lights!"

"Neat," Nancy said.

"On the front it says, 'To Bess.' And

inside it says, 'Happy Holidays from Your Secret Santa.' "

"That's really cool," Nancy said.

"So where's your card?" Bess asked. "What did *you* get?"

Nancy's desk was right next to Bess's. She looked at her desktop. It was bare.

"Nothing," Nancy said with a lump in her throat. "I guess I got nothing!"

2

A Note from Santa

You're kidding!" Bess said to Nancy. "You didn't get anything from your Secret Santa?"

Nancy stared at her desk and shook her head. But she didn't say anything. She didn't want Bess to hear that she was almost ready to cry.

"That's terrible," Bess said.

Nancy nodded and swallowed hard.

Then she thought, Maybe the card fell off my desk.

She looked on the floor. She looked on her chair. She looked inside her desk. She even looked on the desk behind hers.

But she saw nothing except a few tiny sparkles of red glitter on the floor.

"Tell Ms. Spencer," Bess said. "Maybe she forgot to put your card on your desk."

Nancy nodded, but she didn't say anything. She still had a gigantic lump in her throat.

She walked up to Ms. Spencer and stood beside the teacher's desk. She swallowed hard again.

"Yes, Nancy?" Ms. Spencer said, smiling. "What is it?"

"I didn't get a card," Nancy said.

"Really?" Ms. Spencer said. The big smile faded from her face. "Are you sure?"

Without waiting for an answer, Ms. Spencer got up. She walked to Nancy's desk and looked around.

"That can't be right," Ms. Spencer said. "I had a paper bag for each student. Twenty-five bags. I'm sure I put a card on your desk at lunchtime."

"Well, it's gone now," Bess said, joining in.

"Yes, Bess, I see that," Ms. Spencer said. "Nancy, are you sure you didn't find anything on your desk?"

Nancy shook her head.

"All right," the teacher said. "Let me think." She walked back to the front of the room.

While Ms. Spencer was thinking, George came running over.

"Where's your card?" she asked Nancy.

"I didn't get one," Nancy said.

George looked surprised. "That's terrible!" she said. "I can't believe it!"

"Me, either," Nancy said.

Nancy looked around the room. Almost everyone else was talking and laughing. Everyone except Brenda Carlton. She was whispering to another girl. They both had mean smiles on their faces.

"All right. Quiet, everyone," Ms. Spencer said. "George, please go back

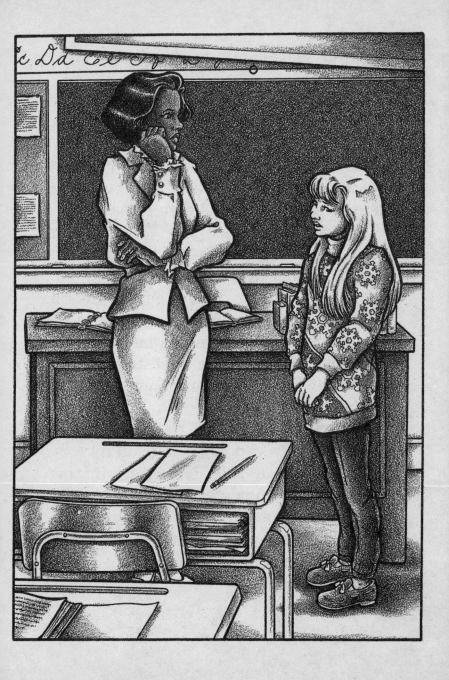

to your seat. Class, we have a mystery to solve."

A mystery? Nancy thought. Hmmm. Maybe this *was* a mystery! Suddenly she felt a little better. Nancy loved to solve mysteries—and she was good at it, too. But this was the first time she had to solve one for herself.

"I want your attention," Ms. Spencer said. It took a while for the class to quiet down. Finally everyone was listening.

"Nancy Drew didn't get a Secret Santa card today," Ms. Spencer began. "But I'm sure I put one on her desk. So I think someone must have taken it by mistake. Does anyone know anything about it?"

The class was silent.

"Well," Ms. Spencer said, "I'm very unhappy about this. If anyone in this class took Nancy's card, I expect that person to give it back right away. Put it in her cubby before the end of the day, and we won't say any more about it. Is that clear?"

No one answered.

"And if Nancy's Secret Santa forgot to bring a card for her, I hope you'll find a way to apologize. Any questions?" Ms. Spencer said.

Jason Hutchings raised his hand. "I have a question," he said.

"Yes, Jason?"

"Do you think her card could have been stolen by aliens from outer space?" he asked.

Everyone laughed. Jason was good at making people laugh.

"No, Jason," Ms. Spencer said. "I don't."

Then Ms. Spencer walked down the aisle to Nancy's desk. "I'm sorry about this, Nancy," she said softly.

"That's okay," Nancy said. But she didn't really mean it.

"I'm proud of you for being such a good sport," Ms. Spencer said. "Some people would be very upset if they didn't get a card today."

That was true, Nancy thought. She looked over at Emily Reeves. Emily had been so excited about the gift exchange. But now Emily wasn't excited at all. She was just sitting at her desk, staring out the window at the snow.

Nancy could see Emily's card lying on her desk. It wasn't very pretty, Nancy thought. It was just a plain folded piece of white paper. Emily's Secret Santa had written "To Emily" on the front in pencil.

Then Nancy sneaked a look at Jason. She wanted to see if he liked the card she had made for him. But he had folded it into a paper airplane and was zooming it around in the air.

That's okay, Nancy thought. The card was made out of silver paper. Perfect for paper airplanes!

Nancy had taped a set of wax teeth inside the card. She saw that Jason was wearing the wax teeth and growling at all his friends.

"Nancy," Ms. Spencer called. "Would you run to the office for me? I need to send this note."

Nancy jumped up. It was fun to go on errands! She was glad the teacher had picked her. It made her feel better.

Nancy walked down the hall to the office with the note in her hand. Then she walked slowly back to class. By the time she reached the room, everyone was doing silent reading.

Nancy picked out a book from the bookshelf. It was a story about a girl who forgot her best friend's birthday.

That's probably what happened to me, Nancy thought as she walked back to her seat. My Secret Santa probably forgot to bring me a card.

Then Nancy saw the note lying on her chair. It was folded into a very small square.

She opened the note. Inside she read:

To Nancy,

I didn't forget about Secret Santa. I made you a beautiful card. It had candy taped to the front. And it had red glitter decorations, too! Someone must have stolen it! Sorry!!

Your Secret Santa

3

Three Suspects, No Clues

Without saying a word, Nancy slipped into her seat. She took out her special blue notebook—the one her father had given her. It had a pocket inside.

Nancy opened the notebook to a fresh page. At the top she wrote: "The Secret Santa Mystery." She drew a line under the words.

Then she wrote: "Christmas card. Stolen during lunch."

Then she wrote one more word.

"Who?" She drew a line under that, too.

Nancy could think of only one person

who would do something like this. Brenda Carlton.

Especially now. Now that Brenda was jealous of Nancy's story in the class newspaper.

Nancy wrote Brenda's name in her notebook, under the word "Who?"

Okay, Nancy thought. If this is a mystery, I'm going to solve it!

She folded up the note she had found on her desk and put it in the pocket of her notebook.

Then she pretended to read her silent reading book. But really she was watching Brenda Carlton.

Nothing happened. All Brenda did was read her own book.

It's hard to solve mysteries during school, Nancy thought. When school was over, Nancy showed the note to George and Bess.

"Well, this proves it," George said as the three friends walked out into the snow. "Someone stole your card. And you've got to find out who—fast!"

"I'm working on it," Nancy said. "I think it might be Brenda Carlton."

"I don't like her," Bess said. "But there are other people who could have done it."

"Who?" Nancy asked.

"Emily Reeves," Bess said. "Remember? She went back into the room before recess was over."

"I don't think she did it," George said. "She was in too much of a hurry to see her own Secret Santa card."

"Well, how about Kyle Leddington?" Bess went on. "He was standing near Nancy's desk when I came in from lunch. Maybe he stole the card."

"Why would he?" Nancy asked.

"To get the candy," George said.

Nancy thought about that as they crossed the street and walked into the park.

"I wonder how much candy was on the card?" Nancy said.

She wished she had the candy now.

Her stomach was growling. She was hungry.

"Maybe it was M&M's, like mine," Bess said.

"Let's not talk about candy," said Nancy.

Then she thought, Maybe when I get home, I can have some hot chocolate. That would make up for not getting candy at school. Sort of.

"Are you going to write down Kyle's name in your notebook?" Bess asked. "And Emily Reeves?"

Nancy nodded. She thought about taking out her notebook right then. But she didn't want to take off her mittens. They were red and white, with snowflakes on them. They matched her sweater. Besides, her hands would get cold.

"Guess what?" Nancy said. "On the way to school today I met Phoebe Archer. She was carrying a *huge* paper bag."

"Do you think she stole your card?" George asked.

"No," Nancy said. "But maybe she brought a really big card for someone."

"No fair," George said. "You're a detective. And now you're going to figure out who everyone's Secret Santa is."

"No, I'm not," Nancy said. "I'm not even *trying* to do that."

"You can't help it," George said. "You figure things out, even when you *don't* try."

Nancy laughed. "Don't worry," she said. "I haven't guessed anything. Maybe Phoebe used a huge bag to hide a tiny card inside. See? I don't know anything about anyone's Secret Santa—yet."

Just then something hit Nancy in the back. A snowball! She turned around and saw a group of boys. Kyle Leddington was one of them. They were having a snowball fight with one another. But they weren't even looking at her.

Then Nancy saw Brenda Carlton coming down the sidewalk.

"Did you throw that snowball at me?" Nancy called.

"Don't be dumb," Brenda said. "Snow-ball fights are for babies—and boys."

"She's the one who's dumb," George said to Nancy. "Snowball fights are for everyone. Watch!"

George picked up a handful of snow. With her back turned, she packed it into a ball. Then she spun around and threw it at Brenda.

Brenda didn't even duck. She just let the snowball hit her on the arm. Then she stuck her nose in the air and kept walking.

"I don't like her," Nancy said.

"Me, either," George said.

"I think she stole your card," Bess said.

"Me, too," Nancy said. "I think."

In the back of her mind Nancy knew that the mystery wasn't over, and the case wasn't closed.

There was still one more thing she needed.

Proof!

4

Bad Luck Lunch

More marshmallows, please," Nancy said to Hannah Gruen. Nancy sat in the kitchen the next morning, drinking hot chocolate before school.

Hannah was the Drew family's housekeeper. She had lived with Nancy and her father for five years—ever since Nancy's mother died.

"Okay," Hannah said, "but these are the last ones. You ate the rest of the marshmallows yesterday—when you had two cups of hot chocolate after school."

"I was hungry," Nancy said. "And thirsty. And cold."

"I don't blame you," Hannah answered. "It was freezing outside. And besides, you deserved a treat. Having your Christmas card stolen! I've never heard of such a thing."

"I'm going to figure out who took it," Nancy said.

"I bet you will," Hannah said with a nod. She turned back to the counter where she was packing a lunch. It was a lunch for Jason Hutchings. Peanut butter sandwich. Potato chips. Apple juice. And Jelly Jets—fruit-flavored jelly candies shaped like jet planes.

"Let's tie a ribbon around the sandwich," Nancy said. "Just to make it special."

"Okay," Hannah said. Then she added, "It's strange to make lunch for someone else and not for you."

Nancy thought about that. "I wonder who's making *my* lunch right now?" she said. "Wouldn't it be funny if it's Jason?"

Hannah laughed. Nancy laughed with her.

Hannah put Jason's lunch in a white bag and wrote his name on it. Then she put the white bag inside a bigger brown one. That way no one would see Jason's name and know that Nancy was his Secret Santa.

Then Hannah drove Nancy to school. It was too cold outside for Nancy to walk.

When Nancy got to class, she put the brown sack on the table in the back of the room.

Twenty other lunches were sitting there already.

I wonder which one is for me? Nancy thought.

She could hardly wait to find out. She hoped she'd get everything on her list of favorite foods. Especially the Panda Crunch bar.

Panda Crunch was a candy bar. It was white and dark chocolate in the shape of a panda bear. And it had crispy things inside. Nancy loved it. She also liked knowing that money from the candy bars went to help save the pandas.

"What are you doing? Snooping around the lunches?" a voice behind Nancy asked.

Nancy spun around. Brenda was standing behind her. "No," Nancy said. "I'm just putting my bag on the table."

"Well, it's cheating to try to find out who your Secret Santa is," Brenda said. "But I won't tell—this time."

"I wasn't snooping!" Nancy insisted.

"That's okay," Brenda said. "I *said* I won't tell. Anyway, here."

Brenda shoved a piece of paper into Nancy's hand. Then she walked away.

Nancy looked at the page. It was a homemade newspaper. The headline at the top said, "Nancy Drew's Christmas Card Stolen."

"What's this?" Nancy asked. But Brenda was already gone.

"It's Brenda's own newspaper," Bess said, coming up beside Nancy. "She's calling it the *Carlton News*. Her dad helped her type it up on their computer last night."

Nancy read the front-page story. It was all about how her card had been stolen. The last line of the story said, "Watch for more news about Nancy Drew's problems—right here in the next issue of the *Carlton News!*"

"Do you know what I think?" Bess said before Nancy was even done reading. "I think she stole your Secret Santa card—just so she'd have something to write about in her newspaper."

For just a moment Nancy felt as if she might cry. "That would be so mean," she said to Bess.

"It would be just like Brenda," Bess said. "George thinks so, too."

Nancy took a deep breath. "Well, we still don't have any proof," she said. "So keep your eyes open."

Bess nodded. "Don't worry, I will."

All morning long Nancy watched

Brenda. But Brenda didn't even leave her seat. Not during math or science or social studies.

Kyle Leddington did. He got up and went out of the room to his cubby. On the way he passed the table where the lunches were. Nancy saw him poke some of the lunch bags as he walked by.

Then it was almost time for lunch. Ms. Spencer sent the whole class to the gym with Mrs. Apple and her third-grade class to play dodgeball. That way she could put out the Secret Santa lunches in private.

For the first round of dodgeball, Nancy was it. She had to stand in the middle of a circle and jump away when the ball came at her. Peter DeSands got Nancy out. He was a good player.

Finally Ms. Spencer came into the gym.

"Time for lunch," she said. She had a twinkle in her eye. "But please clean up before you come back to class."

Everyone hurried out of the gym.

Mrs. Apple walked the students to the rest rooms. Nancy waited in line, then washed her hands as fast as she could. She raced back to the classroom.

"Where's my lunch?" Nancy said the minute she walked through the door. She went to her desk, by the window.

"On your desk," Bess said, without looking up. Her desk was next to Nancy's.

"No, it's not," Nancy said.

Bess looked up. "What do you mean?" she asked.

Just then Nancy heard a familiar laugh. She saw Brenda Carlton standing near the bulletin board by the window.

"Oh, too bad," she said. "Your Secret Santa must really hate you."

"That's a terrible thing to say!" Bess said. She frowned at Brenda. "Can't you see? No one hates Nancy. Her lunch has been stolen!"

"Oh, really?" Brenda said. "Well, that's a shame. I'll bet you really wanted that Panda Crunch bar, too."

"What?" Nancy said.

"I said, I'll bet you really wanted that Panda Crunch bar," Brenda repeated.

Nancy's eyes flashed like fire. She put her hands on her hips. Then she marched over to Brenda. She looked her straight in the eye.

"I have just one question," Nancy said. "If you didn't take my lunch, how do you know there was a Panda Crunch bar inside?"

5

The Chocolate Clues

Are you saying I stole your lunch?"
Brenda asked. She smiled. Nancy
thought Brenda was almost *trying* to
look guilty.

"No," Nancy said. "I'm just asking
you a question. How do you know what
was in my lunch?"

"Maybe I'm your Secret Santa,"
Brenda said with a mean laugh.

Nancy frowned. She hadn't thought
of that. Or at least she hadn't thought
of it that day. Not since she had decided that Brenda was the thief.

"Well, *are* you?" Bess asked. "Are
you Nancy's Secret Santa?"

"No," Brenda said, smiling even more.

"Then how do you know about the Panda Crunch bar?" Nancy asked.

"I *don't* know," Brenda said. "I just saw that you put it on the list on the bulletin board. You asked for a Panda Crunch, so I figured you probably got one. That's all."

"Oh," Nancy said. She felt a little silly. That was a good answer. Nancy hadn't thought of that.

"Well, I'm hungry," Brenda said. "I'm going to get in the lunch line. See you later."

Nancy watched Brenda walk to the front of the classroom. When everyone had lined up, Ms. Spencer would take the class to the lunchroom.

Brenda was carrying her Secret Santa lunch bag under one arm. The bag was very large and full.

That bag is big enough to hold *two* lunches, Nancy thought. Maybe she stole my lunch after all!

Just then George came up to Nancy

and Bess. "Lunchtime!" she said. "What did your Secret Santa give you, Nancy?"

"Nothing," Nancy said.

"Nothing!" George exclaimed. She looked very surprised.

Nancy explained what had happened. George looked over at Brenda. "I think we should watch her," she said.

"Me, too," Nancy said. She grabbed Bess's arm, and all three girls rushed to the lunch line. They stayed close to Brenda as Ms. Spencer took the class to the lunchroom.

To see what Brenda had in her lunch bag, Nancy walked past her table—three times.

On her last trip Nancy saw why Brenda's lunch bag was so big. There was a whole family-size bag of potato chips in it!

"Rats," Nancy said when she got back to her own table. "Maybe she's not the thief."

"I still think she is," George said.

"She's mean. Maybe she stole your lunch and threw it in the trash."

Could be, Nancy thought. She decided to look in the trash after lunch. But just then she was hungry.

Nancy got up and went to find her teacher. When Ms. Spencer heard what had happened, she bought Nancy a lunch in the cafeteria. Macaroni and cheese, and milk.

Yuck, Nancy thought. They have macaroni *every* Thursday! It has brown, crusty things on it. It isn't creamy like Hannah's. And it *isn't* my favorite lunch.

Nancy came back to the table with her tray. "What did you get for dessert from your Secret Santas?" she asked.

Bess had her lunch spread out in front of her.

"Two cupcakes," Bess said. "You can have one if you want, Nancy."

"Thanks, Bess. But where's *your* lunch?" Nancy asked George.

"She already ate it," Bess said.

"Except for the dessert," George said. "I saved it to share with you."

"Thanks," said Nancy. "You guys are the best!"

"Hurry," George said. "I want to go look for clues."

Nancy laughed. She had never seen George so excited about one of her mysteries. Usually it was Nancy who couldn't wait to solve the case.

As soon as they had finished eating, Nancy, Bess, and George sneaked back to the classroom. The room was empty and dark. Nancy felt like a spy.

"We're not supposed to be in here when Ms. Spencer is gone," Bess said.

"I don't care," Nancy said. "I want to solve this case before tomorrow."

"How come?" Bess asked.

"Because tomorrow is the big gift day," George said to her cousin. "If Nancy doesn't catch the thief soon, the person might steal her present again tomorrow. Then she won't get anything at all."

"Oh, right," Bess said.

Nancy started to search. First she looked in the trash can. She found lots of paper towels and all the crumpled-up paper bags. There was no stolen lunch.

Next she looked in Brenda's cubby. She found Brenda's hat, coat, and mittens. But still no lunch.

She even looked in Brenda's desk—without touching anything. Nancy saw some copies of the *Carlton News* but no stolen lunch.

"Now what?" George asked.

"I don't know," Nancy said.

She sat down at her desk and took out her special blue notebook. She turned to a clean page.

She still had three suspects: Brenda, Emily, and Kyle. But she was no closer to finding out which one was the thief.

In her best handwriting Nancy wrote:

Three Facts About Brenda
1. Wrote a newspaper story about me.
2. Asked about my Panda Crunch bar.
3. Had a big lunch.

Big deal, Nancy thought. Her clues were going nowhere!

Just then the bell rang and kids started coming back from lunch. Emily Reeves bounced into the room.

A minute later Jason walked in with his friends. He was eating Jelly Jets. "My lunch was better than yours!" Jason said to his friends in a singsong voice.

"Give me some," Mike Minelli said.

"Yeah. Me, too," Peter DeSands said.

"No way," Jason said. He picked out a big red jet. Then he tilted his head back and waved it around in the air above his open mouth. Mike tried to grab the candy. But Jason flew the jet into his mouth at the last minute.

Nancy felt jealous. Everyone had special treats except her.

"Hey, Jason!" Kyle Leddington called. "Can I have a jet?"

Jason shook his head. "You'd just get it all over your shirt," he said.

All the boys laughed.

That's weird, Nancy thought. Jason didn't usually try to be mean.

Then she looked at Kyle's shirt. There was a big chocolate smear on the front.

So that's why Jason said what he did, Nancy thought. Kyle's shirt was a mess.

And then Nancy realized that the mess was a *brown and white* chocolate smear. Just like the dark and white chocolate in a Panda Crunch bar!

6

The Glitter Clues

Did you see what I just saw?" George said, rushing up to Nancy.

Nancy nodded. "Kyle has chocolate on his shirt."

"And it's *two* kinds of chocolate," George said. "Dark and white. And he was standing beside your desk yesterday when the card was stolen. He's the thief! I know he is. Are you going to ask him about your lunch?"

"No," Nancy said. "I'm going to get some more facts, first."

George made a funny face at Nancy. Nancy knew what it meant. George didn't want to wait. She wanted to catch Kyle right away.

Nancy marched over to the bulletin board. George followed right behind her.

"Look," Nancy said. She pointed to the Secret Santa list. "Kyle asked for a Panda Crunch bar in his lunch, too. That's how he got chocolate on his shirt."

"Oh," George said. Her shoulders slumped. "I thought we had him."

"Nope," Nancy answered with a quick shake of her head.

"Class, it's time to settle down," Ms. Spencer announced as she walked to the blackboard. "Kyle . . . Jason . . . Nancy . . . George . . . please take your seats."

Nancy hurried to her seat and took out her blue notebook. With a red pen she crossed Kyle's name off her suspect list.

He's not the thief, Nancy said to herself. Then she looked up at the bulletin board again.

Wait a minute, Nancy thought. Maybe

Kyle wanted *two* Panda Crunch bars! He could have stolen my lunch to get a second one.

She wrote his name in her notebook again and put two question marks beside it—one for each chocolate bar.

But how could she find out if he ate *two* chocolate bars, Nancy wondered.

For the next half hour Ms. Spencer read a book to the class.

Then it was time for another special event—a Christmas concert. All the classes in the school went to the gym.

Nancy sat in the wooden bleachers with Bess and George. They listened as the sixth graders sang carols and put on a musical play.

But Nancy wasn't really listening to the concert. She was daydreaming about Christmas. And thinking about her Secret Santa.

The next day was the last before Christmas vacation. What if her present was stolen again tomorrow? That would be terrible! This was Nancy's last day to catch the thief.

"Wake up," a voice next to Nancy said.

Nancy looked up. The concert was over, and Brenda Carlton was standing next to her. She was trying to climb over Nancy, so she could get out of the bleachers.

"Are you going to put *this* in your newspaper, too?" Nancy asked.

"No," Brenda said. "Everyone already knows you daydream in school. So it's not news."

Nancy stood up and tried to ignore Brenda. But her face felt hot. That wasn't fair, and Brenda knew it. Nancy wasn't a daydreamer—not usually. Brenda really knew how to make her angry!

With her back to Brenda, Nancy started to follow Bess out of the bleachers. But the bleachers were narrow, so Nancy had to look down to see where she was going.

All of a sudden something red caught Nancy's eye.

Glitter! Red glitter!

"Bess," Nancy said, pointing at the glitter on the narrow wooden steps of the bleachers. "Look!"

"What?" Bess asked.

"Red glitter," Nancy said. "That's what my Secret Santa put on my Christmas card."

"I don't get it," Bess said. "Do you think the card is here in the gym?"

"No," Nancy said. "I think the person who *stole* it was here in the gym— just a minute ago! Glitter sticks to everything. Maybe they had the card with them. Who was sitting here?"

Bess tried to remember. "I think it was either Kyle or Emily," Bess said.

"Okay," Nancy said. She and Bess hurried to join their class. "Let's go!"

By the time Ms. Spencer had led Nancy's class back to their room, the bell was ringing. School was over for the day.

Ms. Spencer dismissed the class. Then she went to the door to watch as the students left. Both Kyle and Emily went to their cubbies.

Nancy raced down the aisle to Emily's seat. Bess was right behind her.

"Look," Nancy whispered. "There's glitter on her chair!"

"Let's look in her desk," Bess said.

Nancy glanced over her shoulder. She didn't want to get caught snooping. But she *did* want to find out if Emily was the thief.

Ms. Spencer had stepped out into the hall. A few students were still in the classroom. But they weren't looking at Nancy.

She knelt down beside the desk and peeked at the papers inside. A plain white folded sheet of paper was on top. Nancy pulled it out. It was the card Nancy had seen on Emily's desk the day before.

On the front, in pencil, the card said, "To Emily." Inside the writing said, "From your Secret Santa. Ha. Ha."

There were no decorations or drawings on it anywhere. It was the plainest card Nancy had ever seen.

Nancy felt sorry for Emily. But she also had a question. If there was no glitter on Emily's card, why was there glitter on Emily's chair?

"What are you doing?" a voice said beside Nancy.

Nancy stood up and saw that Emily had come back. She looked very angry.

"What are you doing in my desk?" Emily asked again.

"I wanted to see your Secret Santa card," Nancy said.

"Why?" Emily asked. "It's really ugly."

"Oh, it's not so bad," Nancy said. She was trying to be nice.

"It's a terrible card, and you know it," Emily said. "And guess what I got for lunch today? A bologna sandwich. I didn't ask for bologna. I hate bologna! And for dessert I got hot pepper chewing gum!"

"At least you got something," Nancy

51

said. "I didn't get any presents. Not yesterday or today."

Emily blushed. Then her eyes darted to her desk. She started to brush away the glitter on her chair. Red glitter was sticking to her dress, too.

Nancy watched Emily carefully and thought about the glitter clues. There was red glitter on Nancy's Secret Santa card *and* on Emily's chair and dress— that meant something.

Either Emily was the thief—or she was the person who made the card in the first place. Maybe she was Nancy's Secret Santa!

"Emily," Nancy said slowly. "Are you my Secret Santa?"

Emily looked surprised. "Why are you asking me that? We're supposed to keep it a secret."

"I know," Nancy said. "But here's what I think. I think either you're my Secret Santa—or you stole my Secret Santa card."

"I did not!" Emily said. "Why would I?"

"I don't know," Nancy said. "But my card had red glitter on it, and you have red glitter on your dress."

"Too bad," Emily said. "I didn't take your card—or eat the candy on it. And you can't prove that I did!"

7

Christmas Joy

Nancy kicked the snow off her boots. Then she climbed into Hannah's car after school.

"Hannah, I've got a problem," Nancy said.

"Close the door," Hannah said with a shiver. "You're letting all the cold air in."

Nancy pulled the car door shut.

"Now," Hannah said, "what's the problem?"

"I've solved another mystery," Nancy said.

"That doesn't sound like a problem," Hannah said.

"But I can't prove that I solved it," Nancy said.

"Ahhh," Hannah said. "That's different. Why don't you tell me all about it?"

As Hannah pulled away from the school, Nancy told her everything. About how her Secret Santa lunch had been stolen. And how she thought Brenda was the thief—until she saw the red glitter on Emily's chair.

"And then Emily said she didn't eat the candy on my card," Nancy said.

"So?" Hannah asked.

"How did she know there *was* candy on my card—unless she stole it?"

"Oh. I see what you mean," Hannah agreed. "But why would Emily take your presents?"

"I've been trying to figure that out," Nancy said. "All I can think of is this. Emily got terrible gifts from her Secret Santa. And I got really nice ones. So she took mine because they were nicer than hers."

"Well, you could be right," Hannah said with a sad shake of her head. "I guess she felt hurt, if her presents were as bad as you say."

"But it's not fair!" Nancy complained. "Why didn't she think about me? I felt really hurt, too, when I didn't get *anything*."

"I know," Hannah said softly. "What she did was wrong." She turned and gave Nancy a warm smile.

"So I want you to call Emily's mother," Nancy said. "Hey, where are we going?"

Nancy looked out the car window and saw that Hannah had turned down Market Street. They were heading toward the mall, not toward home.

"We're going Christmas shopping," Hannah explained. "Your dad is working late tonight. This is the best time for us to pick out a present for him."

"Great!" Nancy said. "We need to get Jason's Secret Santa present for tomorrow, too."

"Oh, yes. I almost forgot," Hannah said.

"But what about Emily?" Nancy asked. "Aren't you going to call her mother?"

"I don't know," Hannah said. "Is that what you really want me to do? Even though you can't prove she stole your gifts?"

Nancy stared out the car window and thought about that. No, she decided. It wouldn't be fair to tell on Emily. Not unless she was sure.

"I wonder who her Secret Santa is?" Nancy said to Hannah.

"Whoever it is isn't very much in the Christmas spirit," Hannah replied.

Nancy drew a Christmas tree in the frost on the car window. Then she drew a picture of some presents, tied with big bows.

Then she pretended the presents were for her—and tried to guess what was inside.

When they got to the mall, Hannah

led the way to a gift shop first. She let Nancy pick out a present for her father. Nancy chose a brown leather pencil cup. It matched the other leather things Carson Drew kept on his desk.

Then Nancy and Hannah ate dinner in the food court. Hannah had Chinese food: noodles with broccoli.

"Yuck," Nancy said. She wrinkled up her nose when she saw Hannah's plate. Nancy didn't like that kind of noodle.

"Yuck, yourself," Hannah said, looking at the hot dog and waffle fries on Nancy's tray.

Finally they went to the toy store. Nancy went to look at the new dolls.

Suddenly, a few feet away, a little girl with red hair started to kick her feet and whine.

"I want that doll! I want that doll, Mommy!" the little girl cried.

"Sorry, Polly, but we aren't buying you anything now," the girl's mother said. "It's too close to Christmas."

"But I want it!" the little girl whined loudly. "Annie got one!"

"Yesterday was Annie's birthday," the girl's mother said. "That's why she got a present."

"I want one, too!" Polly screamed.

Nancy couldn't stop staring. The little girl was yelling at the top of her lungs.

"Come on, Nancy," Hannah said, tugging on Nancy's arm. "We have our own shopping to do."

Nancy followed Hannah to the back of the store. She hunted around for the soft toys. Jason liked squishy balls and foamy sports toys. Finally Nancy settled on a squishy baseball.

"This is the fun part about being a Secret Santa," Nancy said to Hannah. "Picking out a really special gift."

"Too bad Emily's Secret Santa didn't feel that way," Hannah said.

Nancy looked up at Hannah. "You're right," she said.

Just then Nancy heard the little girl's voice again.

"I want it! I want it!" the girl cried out.

"It's too bad when people can't get the things they want, isn't it, Hannah?" Nancy said softly.

"Yes," Hannah agreed. "But people can't always have everything they want."

"I know," Nancy said. "But sometimes they can."

Quickly Nancy turned and ran down one of the aisles.

"Nancy!" Hannah called. "Where are you going? You can't do anything for that little girl!"

"I know," Nancy answered. "But there's just one more thing I want to buy!"

8

Nancy's Secret

When Nancy got to school the next morning, she was carrying two paper bags.

Jason Hutchings and Mike Minelli came up behind her. They were pushing each other from side to side in the hall. Jason bumped into Nancy and stopped.

"Hey, how come you have two bags?" Jason asked.

"It's a secret," Nancy answered.

"I'll bet she got something for the teacher," Mike said. He stuck his tongue out and made a face. "Teacher's pet."

"Nope," Nancy said, shaking her head.

Jason stared hard at the two bags. "Are you a Secret Santa for two different people?" he asked.

"Could be," Nancy said with a mysterious smile.

"Nah," Jason said. "I don't believe you."

Nancy laughed. "Let's go in," she said. "Don't you want to find out who your Secret Santa is?"

Jason walked into the classroom, but he was still staring at the bags. Nancy followed him.

"Okay, class," Ms. Spencer said. "Put your Secret Santa bags on the back table. Then everyone go out into the hall. We're going to open our Secret Santa presents right away today."

"Yes!" some of the kids shouted. "Yay!"

The room was noisy as everyone talked at once. Some kids pushed and shoved. Nancy put her bags on the table and then went back into the hall.

When she got there, George and Bess were just arriving.

"Hurry!" Nancy said. "We're doing Secret Santa right now."

"Great!" George said. Both girls tugged their boots off quickly. Then they ran into the room in their socks. They put their bags on the table.

A minute later they came out. Ms. Spencer was right behind them.

Mrs. Oshida was walking down the hall. Ms. Spencer asked her to keep an eye on the class.

"Is it time for Secret Santa?" Mike called in a loud voice.

"Not yet," Ms. Spencer said. "Nancy? May I see you in the room for a minute?"

Me? Nancy thought. What for?

"What's going on?" George asked in a whisper.

"I don't know," Nancy said.

But as soon as she walked into the

room, she saw Emily Reeves standing next to the teacher's desk.

"Nancy," Ms. Spencer said, sitting down at her desk. "Emily has something to tell you."

Emily looked at her feet.

"Go on, Emily," Ms. Spencer said. "Tell Nancy what you told me."

Emily kept staring down. She said something in a small voice. Nancy couldn't hear the words.

"What?" Nancy asked.

"I just wanted to say I'm sorry," Emily said. "I took your Secret Santa stuff."

"I thought so," Nancy said. "But why did you do it?"

"Will you be mad if I tell you?" Emily asked.

"No," Nancy said. "I don't think so."

"Well," Emily said slowly, "I ran into the room on Wednesday while everyone was still outside. And I saw my card. It was *so* ugly! Then I saw yours. It was

65

beautiful. I took it and ate the candy. I kept the card in my pocket both days."

"But what about yesterday?" Nancy said. "Why did you take my lunch?"

Emily blushed. "I just couldn't help it," she said. "I was first into the room after the concert. When I saw the things in my lunch, I got mad. So I took yours. It was in a pretty bag, with decorations on it. I knew it would be a good lunch."

That's pretty babyish, Nancy thought. But she knew how it felt to want something so badly.

"I'm *really really really* sorry," Emily said. "I'll give you my Secret Santa present. Will that make it okay?"

Nancy smiled. "It's okay," she said to Emily. "I'm glad you told me the truth. You can keep your present." Then she added, "I hope you get something nice."

Emily gave Nancy a grateful smile.

Then Ms. Spencer stood up. She patted Emily on the shoulder. "Good for you, Emily," she said. "And you, too,

Nancy. Now we'd better get started with Secret Santa."

She sent Emily and Nancy out into the hall for a few more minutes. Bess and George were waiting right by the door.

"We heard the whole thing," Bess said.

"I can't believe she stole your gifts!" George said angrily.

Nancy glanced at George. It wasn't like George to be so upset.

"I think she felt left out," Nancy said. "Anyway, she's sorry. So let's not tell anyone."

"Why not?" Bess asked.

"Because if Brenda finds out, she'll put it on the front page of her newspaper," Nancy said. "And I know how *that* feels!"

Bess nodded. "All right," she said.

"Oh, okay," said George.

A moment later Ms. Spencer came to the door. She thanked Mrs. Oshida for watching the class. Then Ms. Spencer called everyone inside.

"Your gifts are on your desks," she told the class.

Everyone rushed into the room. Nancy was so excited. This was the first day she would get a Secret Santa gift! And she couldn't wait to find out who her Secret Santa was.

She ran to her seat and opened her present. It was a necklace. It had colorful fruits dangling all along the chain.

The little card attached to it said, "Merry Christmas. With love from your Secret Santa—George."

"George!" Nancy cried out. "You were my Secret Santa?"

George hurried over to Nancy's desk. "Yes! Do you like the necklace?" George asked.

"I love it! It's great!" Nancy said, giving George a hug. Then Nancy thought for a minute. "No wonder you were so upset when my presents were stolen."

George nodded. "I spent a long time making your card. Hey, there it is!"

Nancy looked down and saw what George was pointing at. On her chair was the red glitter card that George had made. But the candy was missing from the front.

A small note taped to the front said, "I'm sorry I took this. Sorry I ate the candy, too."

"Oh, well," George said. She looked angry for a minute, but then she smiled. "At least she gave it back."

Nancy laughed. "Thanks, again," she said, giving George another hug.

Then George went to see what Bess had gotten from her Secret Santa. Nancy watched from her seat. Almost everyone was happy, including Jason Hutchings. He was throwing his squishy baseball back and forth with Mike Minelli.

Just like Jason, Nancy thought. He didn't even say thank you! But at least she could tell he liked the ball.

Then Nancy glanced over at Emily. She was smiling happily.

"Ooooh! I got two gifts!" Emily cried. "And they're both good ones!"

Nancy saw them on Emily's desk. One was a pretty pink wallet. The other was a tiny stuffed Santa Claus with a pack of toys on his back.

Nancy watched as Emily read the card that came with the wallet.

"Thank you, Peter," Emily said, jumping up and down.

Peter DeSands sat a few seats away from Emily. He got up and walked over to her.

"Do you like it?" he said.

"Oh, I do," Emily said. "Pink is my favorite color!"

"Well, I'm sorry about the bad lunch and card and stuff," Peter said. "I thought it was funny—until I heard you telling Nancy how bad you felt."

"Oh, yeah," Emily said, blushing a little. "Well, anyway, you made up for it with two presents. I love them both."

"Huh?" Peter said. "I didn't give you two presents."

"You didn't?" Emily said. "Then who gave me this Santa Claus doll?"

Peter shrugged.

Emily ran over to Nancy. She brought the Santa Claus with her.

"Nancy," she said. "You're good at solving mysteries, aren't you?"

"Yes," Nancy said.

"Well, I want to know who gave me this present," Emily said. "Can you find out?"

Nancy grinned. "No way," she said.

"But why not?" Emily said. "Are you still mad at me?"

"No," Nancy said. "But I have a feeling the person who gave it to you wants it to be a secret. In fact, I'm sure of it. And some secrets are supposed to stay that way."

Nancy smiled to herself as Emily went back to her desk and sat down. This was turning out to be a good

Christmas after all. And Christmas day hadn't even arrived!

Nancy took out her special blue notebook. She opened it and wrote:

Today I solved the Secret Santa mystery. Now I know why grown-ups always say it's better to give than to receive. It's because when you give someone a present, you end up getting what you want in return—a happy feeling inside.

Case closed.